# The Gryphon Press

*—a voice for the voiceless—*

*These books are dedicated to those who foster compassion toward all animals.*

*To my brood: Dustin, Aaron, and Grayson*
—Sandy De Lisle

*The illustrations in this book are dedicated to my good friend and chicken guru Bonnie White,*
*whose gentle wisdom and passion for poultry have inspired and guided countless kids like Aarón over the years.*
—Amelia Hansen

---

Text set in Bembo by Connie Kuhnz at BookMobile Design and Digital Publisher Services

Printed in Canada

Library of Congress Control Number: 2014953858

ISBN: 978-0-940719-26-2

1 3 5 7 9 10 8 6 4 2

A portion of profits from this book will be
donated to shelters and animal rescue societies.

---

*I am the voice of the voiceless:*
*Through me, the dumb shall speak;*
*Till the deaf world's ear be made to hear*
*The cry of the wordless weak.*

—from a poem by Ella Wheeler Wilcox, early 20th-century poet

written by
Sandy De Lisle

illustrated by
Amelia Hansen

# Hens
for
Friends

My family got Henny, Penny, Fran, Gertrude, Penelope, and Margaret from Mother Hen Chicken Rescue.

I love them all, but Margaret is
my best hen friend. When I sit on
the ground, she jumps into my
lap and tucks her head under my
arm. When I stroke her back, she
makes a funny sound, kind of like
a purring cat.

Sometimes Margaret flies up on my head. The first time she landed on me, I was scared. Now I know it's her way of telling me she likes me.

I put my hands on either side of her body so she won't fall off my head. Then I walk around my backyard. I think she likes the view from up high.

Mom laughs and says, "Margaret's on top of the world, Aarón."

I say, "I am too."

We almost didn't get to have our hens because there were people who didn't want chickens living in our city. At the town hall meeting, a lady in front of us said, "Chickens will bring rodents—and they also carry diseases!" Luckily, the city council still passed the law, allowing each family to keep up to six hens.

Mice and rats haven't bothered us or our chickens because we put our chickens' feed in covered containers and keep their coop clean.

And when I am done cleaning the coop or playing with the hens, I always wash my hands so I don't get sick from any germs they might have.

Every morning we let the hens out of their barn into their yard. We fenced in a small area for them to run in—and we even put a roof over part of it so hawks can't swoop down and grab one of the hens when we're not looking.

While Mom fills the hens' feeders with chicken feed and fresh water, I get to gather their eggs.

I handle the eggs very carefully so they don't break. Most days there are five or six eggs to collect.

I always keep
a pencil in my
pocket so I can
mark Margaret's
eggs with an "M."

Mom says our hens' eggs are unfertilized because we don't have a rooster. That means there are no baby chicks in the eggs.

When I finish collecting their eggs, I like
to spend time watching the chickens. They
often chase bugs in the grass
and peck at things.

Sometimes they even peck at my shoelaces.
Maybe they think the laces are worms.

Dad hung a wind chime in the hens' pen, and
when one of them pecks at it, all the other hens
come running. They squawk and jump around like
they're having a big dance party.

The hens love to take dust baths. They find a nice sunny patch of dirt, dig a shallow hole with their feet and wings, and flop down in it. Pretty soon dirt is flying everywhere! Mom says they are getting bugs off themselves.

"I wish I could take a bath in the dirt," I say. "It sure looks like fun!"

"Most hens don't get to take dust baths," Mom says.

"Don't other hens like dust baths?" I ask.

"All hens love to take dust baths, Aarón, but most hens live on very large farms in small cages that they share, and they never get to go outside," Mom explains. "Our hens are lucky to be with us."

"Why does the farmer treat them like that?" I ask. "That doesn't sound like a farm to me."

"In those factory farms, they have thousands of hens to care for," Mom says.

"Well, then, they shouldn't keep so many hens," I say.

"I agree," Mom says.

As Mom scoops up the hens' poop from the yard, I think about how smelly a factory farm must be with all the poop and pee from thousands of chickens.

We put our hens' poop in a big plastic container called
a composter. After a few weeks, the bacteria break it down
and it becomes soil. We put the soil in our garden, where it
helps our tomatoes, zucchini, and broccoli grow.

The man at the feed store says that if we take good care of our hens, they will live a long time. I will take care of them always, even when they are too old to lay eggs.

After dinner, I help Dad put Margaret and the others
to roost for the night. My little brother, Eduardo, is too
young to help. He chases the hens and scares them.
But not me. I know just how to act around them—
calm and quiet.

Sometimes if we are late putting the hens to bed,
they put themselves to sleep. Dad says
they are so smart, they can tell time
without using a clock.

Today we are using two of the eggs from our hens to make a birthday cake for Eduardo. Mom lets me add them to the batter. I make sure to use Margaret's eggs so Eduardo's cake is extra special.

I tell him, "Margaret helped make your cake!"

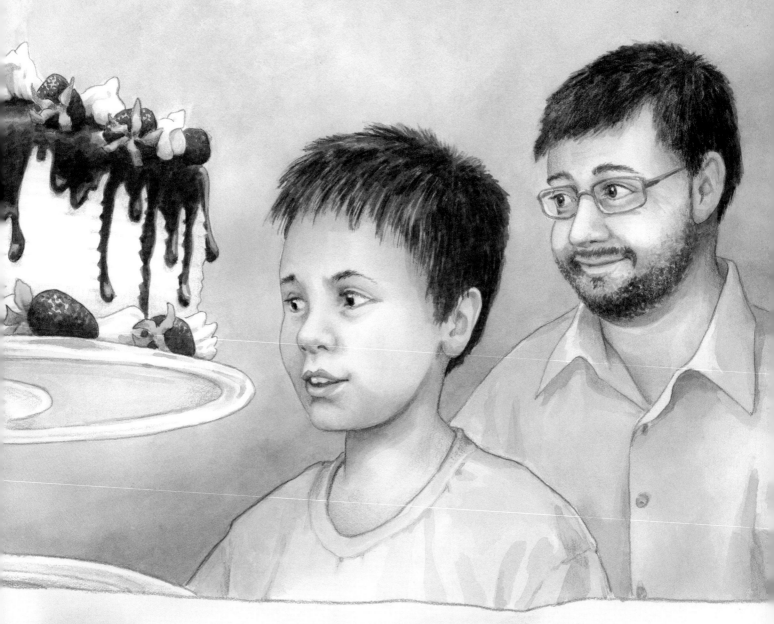

He laughs at me and shouts, "No!"

I want to stick my tongue out at him, but instead I say in my most grown-up voice, "Someday you'll understand how magnificent it is to have hens for friends."

When the other hens aren't
looking, I give Margaret a
piece of strawberry from
Eduardo's birthday cake.
She gobbles it right up.
"You're special, Margaret,"
I whisper in her ear. She makes
a squawk that sounds just
like "You are too."

Mom's right: our hens
are lucky to have us.
But I feel lucky to
have them too,
especially Margaret.

# Having Hens for Friends

### The Fun Part

Chickens make great companions. Some chickens show affection by cuddling up with or "hugging" their humans. Recent research shows that not only are chickens smart about being chickens, but they can also understand human concepts like recognizing numbers and showing empathy.

Another benefit of having hens is that they can lay up to one egg every few days until around the age of four. If you don't have a rooster, the eggs will be unfertilized, meaning there is no chick embryo inside. Therefore, if you eat eggs, you can enjoy your hens' eggs without harming a baby chick or having to worry about whether the hen who laid your eggs was treated humanely.

Remember that after your hen stops laying eggs, she will still need a loving home for up to ten or more years, because many hens live to be fifteen years old or older.

### What You Need to Know

Check with your city or town to make sure hens are allowed. Even municipalities that allow hens have very strict regulations on how many you can legally keep and where they can be housed on your property.

Although chickens make lovely additions to your family, they can bring unwanted visitors, including rodents, predators like hawks, foxes, and coyotes, and even salmonella. Take steps to protect your hens and yourself:

- Store chicken feed in airtight containers.
- Sweep up the barn and chicken yard, making sure to keep them free of food residue and chicken droppings as much as possible.
- Change the hens' straw or other bedding frequently.
- Lock the hens up at night in a predator-proof coop and put netting on outdoor enclosures to prevent aerial attacks from hawks or other large predatory birds.
- Wash your hands with soap and water after handling the chickens and the eggs to prevent salmonella contamination.

If you are not prepared to take these precautions, having a hen for a friend may not be a good idea for you.

### Where to Find a Hen Friend

Rescuing a hen from a chicken rescue or animal shelter is the ideal way to go. Don't buy chickens from a breeder, because that will create a demand for more chickens to be raised—and there are already too many older hens without homes.

Check with your local animal shelter, or search for "birds" on petfinder.com to find adoptable chickens in your area. You can also try www.sanctuaries.org.

### Resources

http://www.humanesociety.org/animals/chickens/tips/adopting_chickens.html

http://www.cdc.gov/features/salmonellapoultry/

*Things to Consider When Purchasing Eggs*

http://www.humanesociety.org/issues/confinement_farm/facts/guide_egg_labels.html